Hansel & Gretel

Once upon a time, deep in the woods, lived a woodcutter with his wife and his two small children, Hansel and Gretel. Their father loved them dearly, but their stepmother wasn't nearly so kind. She wanted nothing more than to be rid of the children.

The woodcutter was very poor and had very little food to feed his family. One day, his wife confronted him. She insisted that the only way that they could survive would be to get rid of the children. She came up with a plan to abandon Hansel and Gretel deep in the forest. Reluctantly, their father agreed.

The woodcutter and his wife did not know that the children were in the next room, and had overheard the terrible plan. Gretel was scared and turned to her brother.

"What will we do?" she cried helplessly.

"Don't worry, Gretel. I'll think of something," said Hansel.

That evening, Hansel thought of a plan. After everyone else had gone to bed, he quietly snuck outside. Hansel collected as many white pebbles as he could find and placed them in his pockets. When his pockets were full, he crept quietly back to bed and fell asleep.

At the break of dawn, their stepmother woke Hansel and Gretel.

"Get out of bed!" she yelled sternly. "You'll be helping your father cut wood in the forest today."

She shoved the children out the door and locked it behind them.

The children obediently followed their father through the forest. As they walked, Hansel secretly dropped the pebbles from his pocket. If they became lost in the forest, he knew that the pebbles would lead them back home.

After walking for a long time, their father stopped in a clearing.

"Children," he said, "I need you to collect as many twigs as you can. I am going to cut wood nearby. I'll be back soon to get you."

And with that, their father left them.

Hansel and Gretel did as they were told, and collected all the twigs they could find. Then, they sat down on the forest floor to wait for their father.

When dusk fell, Hansel and Gretel began to get worried. They sadly realized that their father was not coming back for them.

"We're lost!" Gretel sobbed.

"Not quite," Hansel replied, pointing to a white pebble at her feet. "I dropped these pebbles while we walked. Now all we have to do is follow them back home!"

Just as Hansel had planned, the pebbles led the children right back to their doorstep.

When their stepmother saw that Hansel and Gretel had returned, she was furious! She sent them straight to bed without dinner. They were very hungry, but the children obeyed her. They were happy just to have a warm bed to sleep in.

The next morning, their stepmother woke the children. She ordered them to join their father outside, just as they had done the day before, and gave them each one slice of bread. Hansel had been too tired to collect pebbles the night before, so he decided to drop breadcrumbs along the path instead.

This time, the woodcutter led Hansel and Gretel even deeper into the forest. He asked them to collect stones and promised he would come back for them. As they waited for their father to return, the tired children closed their eyes, and soon they were fast asleep.

The next morning, Hansel woke up and discovered that all of the breadcrumbs had disappeared.

"The birds must have eaten them," Gretel said sadly.

As they tried to think of a new plan, a bird landed nearby and sang a sweet song. The curious children followed it, and soon found themselves standing in front of a magnificent gingerbread house!

The hungry children couldn't resist the delicious aroma, and soon began to nibble on the walls. Suddenly, the door creaked open and an old woman stood before them.

"Hello, children. If you're hungry, there are plenty more treats inside the house!" she said kindly, beckoning them inside.

When they entered, the children found a wonderful feast laid out on the kitchen table. There were plates piled high with cookies, cakes, and pies. There was more food than they had ever seen before!

"Don't be shy. Eat as much as you like," the old woman said.

Hansel and Gretel began to eat.

16

The children had no idea that the kindly old woman was really a witch in disguise. She had spent a long time making her house, and was angry that Hansel and Gretel had eaten so much. The witch planned to cook the children… and eat them!

After the children ate, the witch locked Hansel in a cage.

Over the next few days, Gretel was forced to do chores around the house. The witch continued to feed Hansel.

"I'll make you nice and plump, and then I'll eat you!" she cackled.

From time to time, she would ask Hansel to stick his finger out of the cage. Then, she would pinch it to see how fat he was getting.

Gretel soon realized that the old witch was nearly blind.

"Hansel, the next time she asks to feel your finger, hold out this chicken bone," Gretel instructed. "If she thinks you're too skinny, she won't eat you!"

From then on, each time the witch asked how fat he was, Hansel would give her the chicken bone to pinch.

The witch grew impatient. Finally, she couldn't take it anymore.

"Skinny or fat, I'm cooking you today!" she told Hansel. "Gretel, light the oven!"

Gretel sweetly asked the witch to help her. As the witch leaned in to light the oven, Gretel pushed her in and slammed the door shut! Then, Gretel ran over to the cage and freed Hansel.

As they were about to head out the door, Hansel noticed something glittering in the corner of the room. It was a treasure chest full of gold coins!

Together, the children carried the chest down the forest path. They followed the same chirping bird that had led them to the gingerbread house many weeks ago. This time, the bird led them through the woods, right back to their father's doorstep.

When they arrived, they found their father alone in the house. He had finally realized that his wife was terribly wicked, and had sent her away!

When he saw them, their father scooped Hansel and Gretel up in his arms. He had missed them so much!

"Papa, we have a surprise for you!" Hansel said, revealing the chest full of coins.

Their father was overjoyed, and they lived happily ever after.